SECRET RADIO MESSAGES

JOSEPH CLARO

To Tasha, Nikki, Noel, Danielle, and Chris

Photographs by Richard Hutchings

The editors wish to thank Ray Cerbone (WA2MZX) for providing technical assistance and advice.

ISBN 0-590-35194-X

12 11 10 9 8 7 6 5 4 2/9

31

CHAPTER 1

Have you ever tried to describe how you feel about somebody? I mean, without getting all corny and mushy and everything? I have. I've tried to tell some people how I feel about my friend. And I don't think anybody understands what I'm trying to say. Not even my mother and father. And they understand almost everything I tell them.

Well, I'm going to try again. I'm going to try

explaining why I don't ever expect to have another friend like Yuke.

I know. That's a pretty strange name for a kid. But Yuke was a pretty strange kid.

He moved in about two years ago. The house three doors away from mine had been empty for about three months. Then one day, we saw a moving van pull up. Pete, Benny, and I were pretty interested in that. So we sat on the curb to watch.

A car pulled up behind the moving van. The driver was a woman. She got out and started talking to the moving men. They talked for a few minutes. Then she unlocked the front door of the house and went inside.

It was a hot day, around the end of August. Those moving men were going to have a hard time working in that heat. They opened the side door of the truck. Then they started carrying furniture into the house.

I don't know why we sat there watching them. I mean, I have seen people move in before. There isn't anything very exciting about it. I guess we were waiting to see if the new family had any interesting things. They might have a pool table, or a pet shark or something. But all we saw was very ordinary things — beds, lamps, tables, things like that.

We did spot a bicycle on its way into the garage. And it was a boy's bike. So that meant they had a son. But you can't be sure how old a kid is by looking at his bike. So the kid might have been eight or nine, or he might have been fifteen.

Anyway, after a while I got bored watching chairs and bookcases. So I told Pete and Benny I would see them later. Then I got up and went into my house.

After lunch I went back outside. Benny and Pete were still sitting there, watching the moving men. I walked over and sat down beside them again. I said, "I didn't miss anything, did I?"

Benny said, "Yeah, you did."

"Yeah?" I said. "What?"

"The new kid," Benny said. "He came in a car with his father about ten minutes ago."

"No kidding?" I said. "Did you get a chance to talk to him?"

"No," Pete said. "He just looked at us and went inside."

"How old is he?" I asked.

"How should I know?" Pete said. "I just told you we didn't talk to him."

"Well, you saw him, didn't you?" I said. "How old did he look?"

Benny said, "He's about 13 or 14. And he has a mini-bike. You missed that, too."

"Maybe he'll be out later," I said. "Then we can see what kind of guy he is."

The movers were carrying in some of the last boxes of stuff. None of us could see any reason for hanging around. So we wandered over to my house to watch television. Pete and Benny got a little tired of watching the ballgame after a while. So they both went home.

A little while after that, I got bored with the game. I went outside to see what was happening.

What was happening was that the new kid was up on his roof with some wire.

CHAPTER 2

I walked over to his house and looked up at him. He didn't see me, because he was looking at the wire he was holding. So I called up to him, "Hey! What are you doing up there?"

He was squatting to keep his balance. He

turned his head around and looked at me. Then he smiled.

"I'm trying to get an antenna up," he said.

"An antenna for what?" I asked.

"My radio," he answered. "I have a ham radio."

"Need any help?"

He slid to the edge of the roof. "Sure," he said, "I could use some help."

There was a ladder propped against the side of the house. He stepped onto it and climbed down.

"I'll go inside and get the antenna. My name's Yuke." He held out his hand. "What's yours?"

"Greg," I said. "I live in the brown house on the corner." Then I shook hands with him. I felt kind of silly doing that. I mean, kids don't shake hands when they meet. But I told you Yuke was a strange kid.

"Hiya, Greg," he said. "I'll be out in a minute."

It wasn't until he was gone that I realized what a weird name he had. "Yuke?" I said to myself. "What kind of name is that?"

He came out of the house with an antenna. I said, "Did you say your name was Yuke?"

"Yeah," he said. "Short for Euclid. That's a Greek name."

"Euclid? I never heard that name before. Are you Greek?"

He put down the antenna and smiled at me. "No," he said. "It's what you might call an oddball name. My parents thought it would be funny to have a kid named Euclid."

"It probably causes you all kinds of trouble," I said.

He was working with the wire and the antenna. "What do you mean?" he asked.

"Your name," I said. "I used to know a kid named Armbruster once. Everybody made fun of him. He used to get into fights all the time because of his name. Doesn't that happen to you?"

He looked at me for a couple of seconds. Then he said, "No. No, it doesn't."

I couldn't tell you what it was. But the way he looked at me made me realize *why* he never had any trouble about his name. He looked like the kind of guy you wouldn't make fun of, no matter what his name was.

He seemed very sure of himself. But he

seemed sure in a different kind of way. I guess you could call it pride. But it wasn't the kind of pride that would make him brag. He just believed that he was pretty good. And he probably didn't have to prove it to anybody. I liked that. That's the way I wanted to be myself.

"How old are you, 14?" I asked.

"No, 12," he said. "You?"

"Twelve," I said. "You in the seventh grade?"

"Yep," he said. He was sitting on the ground. He was trying to connect the wire to the antenna.

"Me too," I said.

He smiled again. Then he stood up and said,

"I think I've got this connected now. Want to come up and give me a hand?"

"Sure," I said. I climbed up the ladder after him. Then I held the antenna while he nailed the wire in place. After that, we both fastened the antenna with some braces he had in his pocket.

When we got back down, he said, "Thanks a lot, Greg. That would have taken me hours."

"That's OK," I said. "It was fun."

It really was, too. I mean, I really enjoyed helping him. Part of the fun was being up on the roof. My mother would never let me go up on our roof. I was lucky she didn't happen to look out the window while we were up there.

Yuke said, "Listen, I'm going to try the radio to make sure it works. Want to come in with me?"

"Sure," I said. I had never even seen a real ham radio set before. But I didn't want to tell him that.

We went inside, and Yuke introduced me to his mother. She offered me a glass of milk, but I said no. She seemed nice enough.

Yuke and I went up to his room. All the furniture was in there, but it was just sort of jammed in. I guess the movers didn't care where they put it, as long as they got it in the right room.

Yuke opened his window, and I saw a wire

dangling from the roof. He connected it to a wire coming out of his radio. Then he said, "OK, let's give it a try."

He fooled around with the dials for a few seconds. Then we heard some static. I was amazed. I mean, I didn't know the first thing about radios. The radio was working, and I had helped him set it up.

Before I knew it, he was talking with some guy. They exchanged call numbers. Yuke told the guy he had just moved into a new house, and he was trying out his set. The guy told Yuke to call him every once in a while. Then they both signed off.

I just sat there watching. It sounds stupid, but I felt like I was in the middle of a space movie. As I said, radios were a big mystery to me.

Yuke turned the radio off. Then he said, "OK, good. We do nice work, don't we, Greg?"

"Yeah," I said. "We sure do. Hey, listen, can I try making a call sometime? I mean, I've never worked one of these before. In fact, I don't know anything about ham radios."

"You can make a call right now," he said. He flicked a switch, and the radio was on again. Yuke had to help me a little, but I made contact after a few seconds.

It was really silly. Here I was with this microphone in front of me. And someone was listening, waiting for me to say something. And

all I could say was "Hello?"

Yuke laughed. He turned the radio off. Then he said, "I'll have to teach you some things. There's a certain way of talking on ham radios. It's almost like learning another language."

"Will you teach me?" I asked.

"Sure," he said. "It's almost time for dinner. Want to start tomorrow?"

"OK," I said. "See you tomorrow." I walked home wondering how much a ham radio would cost. I was also thinking about this guy Yuke. He

was really something special. He knew all about ham radios. I knew nothing about them. And all he said was "I'll have to teach you some things."

Most guys I know wouldn't have done it that way. They would have made a big deal about how much they knew. They would have told me how hard it is to learn. Yuke just said, "I'll have to teach you some things."

He didn't try to act smart, even though he knew something I didn't know. Like I said, he was something special.

CHAPTER 3

After I finished dinner, I didn't know what to do. It was still light out. I was going to call Benny. Then I heard the front doorbell ring.

I opened the door, and Yuke was there.

"Hi," he said. "Doing anything?"

"Nope," I said. "You want to come in?"

"No, thanks," Yuke said. "I was just going to make some calls. I thought maybe you could come over. I mean, instead of waiting until tomorrow."

"Great!" I said. "Be with you in a minute."

I went to the kitchen and told my mother I would be down the street. Then Yuke and I went to his house. We went right up to his room. Yuke sat down in front of the radio.

"I don't really know where to start," he said. "There are a lot of things you have to learn."

"Why don't you make a call?" I said. "But tell me what you're doing. Then maybe I can try it."

"OK," he said. "Now, this is the transceiver. It does two things: it transmits messages — sends them out — and it receives messages. When you press the switch on the microphone, the transmitter section goes on and you can talk. When you let the switch up, the receiver section goes on and you can listen."

He turned the transceiver on. We heard somebody talking, but the voice was very low.

"We're getting something," he said. "But we have to tune in better." He began turning the main tuning knob. Then we realized that there were two voices.

"Let's listen in," Yuke said. "I want you to hear what a ham conversation sounds like."

We listened for a couple of seconds. Then I said, "Hey, I know that voice. That's the kid you were talking to this afternoon."

"Yeah, that's right," Yuke said. "Phil Gorman."

Then we heard Phil say, "You know, you can't really get away with this."

The other voice sounded like an older guy. He

said, "That's nothing for you to worry about. You just do what I tell you to do. If you don't, you know what happens."

Then Phil said, "Yeah, I know." He sounded scared. He said, "How long are you going to keep me in this thing?"

"As long as we can use you," the other voice said. "You just be a good boy, and keep those messages coming. Then nothing will happen to you."

"OK," Phil said. "I'll keep them coming."

"Good," the other guy said. "Now, you be ready at 3:30 tomorrow afternoon. That's when you'll get the message on the phone. Then call me at 4:00. And you better be sure you get the message right. You hear me?"

"I hear you," Phil said. "I'll call you tomorrow at 4:00."

"That's a good little boy," the other guy said. "Just do exactly as you're told, and you'll be all right."

Then they both signed off.

Yuke turned off the transceiver.

"I wonder what that was all about," I said.

"It sounded weird, didn't it?" Yuke said.

"It sure did," I said. "Phil sounded scared silly."

"I would have been scared, too," Yuke said. "I mean, did you hear the way that other guy was talking to him?"

"I heard," I said. "What do you think is going on?"

"I don't know," Yuke said. "Maybe I should call

him again. Maybe he will tell me what's going on."

"I don't think so," I said. "I'll bet he's too scared of that other guy."

"I guess you're right," Yuke said. "But if something is wrong, we ought to try to help Phil."

"How can we do that?" I asked.

"Maybe we can find out what's wrong," Yuke said. "Maybe we can tune in for that message tomorrow. Then we might be able to figure out what's happening."

"OK," I said. "We'll wait until tomorrow."

"Yeah," Yuke said, "that's what we'll do. Now let me show you how this thing works."

So I had my first lesson in working a ham radio. Yuke helped me make a call. I talked with a girl who lived about 300 miles away from us. I got a kick out of that. But I don't think I learned much. I was having too much fun to pay attention to what Yuke was explaining.

Besides, I kept thinking about Phil. I'm pretty sure Yuke was thinking about him, too. But we didn't say anything about it until I was ready to go home.

"See you tomorrow," I said.

"Right," Yuke said. "We have to pick up a message tomorrow afternoon."

We both smiled. I guess we both had the feeling that this was going to be exciting.

CHAPTER 4

That night I had some trouble getting to sleep. I kept thinking about Phil. I was trying to figure out what was happening. But I couldn't make any sense out of it. So, after a long time, I finally got to sleep.

When I woke up, I started thinking about it all over again. I couldn't get it out of my mind. Pete and Benny came to my house at about ten in the morning. I took them over to meet Yuke. Then we all went to the playground to play some basketball.

Yuke didn't tell Pete and Benny about the call we had heard. So I figured I'd better not mention it, either.

Pete and Benny went home for lunch. After they left, I brought up the subject again.

"Yuke, how come you didn't tell the guys about Phil?"

He looked surprised. "I thought *you* didn't want them to know," he said. "I was having trouble *not* saying anything."

We both laughed. "They will flip when they hear about it," I said.

"Yeah," Yuke said. "We can tell them when they get back from lunch."

We started walking home. Neither of us said anything for a while. Then I said, "Yuke, I think maybe we'd better not tell Pete and Benny."

Yuke looked at me. "Whatever you say," he said.

I could tell he didn't understand. I mean, he didn't know why I didn't want the guys to know. But he agreed anyway. I liked that.

I was glad he didn't ask me why. I couldn't have given him an answer. I just didn't want anybody to know about this except Yuke and me.

Pete and Benny came back after lunch. But it was too hot to do much of anything. So we just hung around near my house.

At about 3:00, Benny said, "I'll see you guys later — when the sun goes down."

"Wait," Pete said, "I'll come with you."

After they left, we went up to Yuke's room. We had almost an hour to kill. So Yuke started explaining about Morse code. That looked like something I would never be able to learn.

He gave me a list of letters. Next to each letter was the code — dots and dashes. Then he showed me how to tap out some letters, like S and N. Before long, I was tapping them out myself.

"You have to learn the whole code," Yuke said. "They give you a test on it when you go for a license."

"I'll need a lot of practice," I said.

"I'll give you the practice," he said.

He taught me a few more letters. Then I looked at the clock near his bed. "It's ten to four," I told him.

"Yeah, I know," he said. "I've been watching that clock like a hawk."

He put the telegraph key aside. Then he tuned the transceiver in on Phil. We had to wait a few minutes. Then we heard Phil placing a call.

Yuke copied down the call number. "We might be able to use this sometime," he said to me.

"Right," I said. I didn't know what we would ever use it for. But it did seem like the right thing to do.

Phil's contact received the call. He said, "Go ahead, Shakespeare."

"Shakespeare?" I said. "What does that mean?"

"Shhh!" Yuke said. "Let's just listen."

"This message is from the director," Phil said. "The play is all ready. But he needs some props. The three leading actors have to go to the theater. Be sure they bring their equipment."

It sounded weird, all right. But there was something else. Phil was talking very slowly. It was almost as though he were talking in a foreign language. Or a code. Not the Morse code with dots and dashes, but a code with words.

"Which theater are we using?" the other guy asked.

Phil answered, "The one at 613 West Street. Tell them the play begins at 8:00 tonight!"

Yuke wrote down the address. Then the older guy said, "Good boy, Shakespeare. You do nice work. I'll call you tomorrow." And he signed off.

Yuke turned off the transceiver. He sat down on the edge of his bed. "Now what?" he said.

"I don't know," I said. "I still can't figure out what's going on. Can you?"

"No," Yuke said. "But that sure was a strange conversation. I mean, it didn't sound like conversation."

"I know," I said. "You know what it sounded like to me?"

"What?"

"It sounded like code," I said. "The guy called him Shakespeare. And Phil was talking about a play, and a director, and actors, and props. I'll bet it's some kind of code."

"If it is a code," Yuke said, "those guys are breaking the rules. Coded messages are forbidden on ham bands." He paused and then asked, "Do you think we should do something?"

I said, "Yes, I think we should do something. And I think I know what we should do."

"Yeah," Yuke said, smiling. "Me too."

"We're going to a theater tonight," I said. "At 613 West Street."

"Right," Yuke said. "And you know something? I have a feeling we're going to be the only ones in the audience."

"I'd better get home," I said. "See you after dinner."

"OK," Yuke said. "We'll take our bikes."

CHAPTER 5

Yuke came by for me at 6:30 that night. We told our parents we were going to the school gym. That was true. But there was something we didn't tell them. We didn't say we would be leaving there at 7:30.

When we got to the gym, we met some guys who were in my class. We played basketball for a while, three guys on a side. At 7:15, Yuke sat down on the sidelines.

"I've had enough," he said. "Guess I'll be going."

"Me too," I said. We started walking toward the door. Then I spotted some trouble. Jamie Roberts and his friends were coming in.

Jamie and his friends went to the same school I did. They were the kind of guys you stayed away from. They did things like taking lunch money from fifth graders. They pushed people around a lot in school. Nothing really dangerous. They just always seemed to be looking for a fight.

And that's what they were doing right now.

"Hello, new kid," Jamie said.

Yuke stopped walking. "You talking to me?" he asked.

"You're the only new kid here," Jamie said.

"My name's Yuke."

"Your name's what?" Jamie said. Then he started laughing. His friends did, too.

"Look, fella," Yuke said, "I'm in a hurry. If you feel like playing games, I don't have time right now."

It looked like a fight. I guess I wanted it to be a fight.

"No game," Jamie said. "I was just wondering if you could take care of yourself."

Yuke started walking toward the door, and I followed him. "Some other time," Yuke said. "I'll take care of myself some other time."

As we walked out the door, I heard Jamie and his friends laughing. I was a little embarrassed for Yuke's sake.

"You should have fought him," I said.

"What for?" Yuke asked. "We have an appointment, remember?"

"I know," I said. "But now he's going to think you're afraid."

Yuke stopped walking. He turned to face me. He looked a little confused. "What do I care what he thinks?" he said. "I don't even know who he is."

"Everybody else knows who he is," I said. "And he'll noise it around that you walked away from a fight."

"So?" Yuke asked.

"So," I said, "everybody will think you're afraid." I felt a little stupid saying that. I didn't know why, but that's how I felt.

"I want to explain something to you," Yuke said. He was frowning. But I don't think he was angry. He was just very serious.

"OK," I said. "Go ahead."

"I know I'm not afraid," he said. "And you know it, too. Don't you?"

"Sure," I said. "But everybody else — "

"I don't care about everybody else," he said. "I don't know them. And they don't know me. So how can they know if I'm afraid?"

"But they'll think you are," I said quietly.

"That's their problem," he said. "I can't worry about what everybody believes. I only worry about the people who matter."

I thought about that for a few seconds. Then I smiled at Yuke. He smiled back.

"Let's go," he said. "The show is about to start."

We got on our bikes and rode to West Street.

When we got to 613, we weren't surprised to find that it wasn't a theater. It was a big warehouse. There was no one around, and the buildings nearby looked deserted too. We chained our bikes to a lamppost two blocks away. Then we walked back to the warehouse.

It was a big old dirty building. It really looked spooky. I was beginning to think we were making a bad mistake.

"Yuke?" I said. I almost whispered it.

"What?"

"Maybe this isn't the right place," I said.

"No," Yuke said. "This is it — 613 West Street. Let's look around. Maybe we can get inside."

We started walking around the building. There was only one door. It was in the front of the building. It was big enough for trucks to drive into. On one side of the building we found a broken window.

"We can get in through here," Yuke said. He reached inside the broken pane. He unlocked the window from the inside. Then he took his hand out and pushed the window up. He climbed into the warehouse. I followed him.

CHAPTER 6

When we were both inside the warehouse, Yuke closed the window again. Then we looked around. It was dark, because two walls had no windows and the windows in the other two walls were too dirty to let in much light. There were some wooden crates and big cardboard boxes piled near us, but the rest of the space looked empty. On the other side of the warehouse, a light shone under a closed door.

All of a sudden, the door opened. The light came shining out from a small room. Yuke and I jumped behind a big box.

We looked around the side of the box. Two men came out of the little room. They were talking. But we couldn't hear what they were saying. They started walking toward us.

"Yuke," I whispered, "this is crazy! What if they find us?"

All he said was "Shhh!"

The men were getting closer. My heart was beating fast. I was sure they would hear it. I had never been so scared in my life!

They stopped when they reached the big door in the front. They were close enough for us to hear them now.

"It's eight o'clock," one of the men said. "Time to open up the store."

The other one laughed. He said, "Let's just hope the kid got the message to Slim."

They opened the big door. The light from outside made the area around the door a little brighter. Yuke and I crouched down a little more.

Then we heard a car. We looked out from behind the box. The driver stopped when he got inside the big door. He turned his headlights on. One of the men said to him, "Just pull it up all the way in the back." We watched the car roll into the warehouse and across the empty space. When it reached the back wall, the headlights went out.

Then another car pulled in. The men told the driver to park it next to the first one. Right after that, a third car drove up. It was beginning to look like a parade. In 10 minutes, there were 15 cars parked in that warehouse.

We heard the big door close. The two men walked to the back, where all the cars were parked. One of them talked to the drivers.

"Everybody was right on time," he said. "This thing runs better every week. Now, you all know where to pick up your money. Your contact will meet you tomorrow. Same place as last week. Did anybody have any trouble this week?"

"Yeah," one of the drivers said. "I couldn't get this thing started. Then a cop came over. He asked me if I needed any help."

They all broke out laughing at that. It sounded weird. I mean, all those guys laughing. And the sound was echoing all over the warehouse. It was like being in a horror movie.

While the laughing was going on, Yuke leaned over to me. "Car thieves," he whispered. "It's a whole ring of car thieves."

The laughing died down. "OK, boys," the man said. "You get paid tomorrow. And we'll see you again next week. Happy hunting. You leave here one at a time."

"Let's get out of here," Yuke said.

"Now?" I said.

"Come on," Yuke said. "We'll crawl over to that broken window."

CHAPTER 7

As soon as I finished breakfast the next morning, I went to Yuke's house. We sat in his backyard. We had some things to talk about.

"We've turned up some pretty interesting stuff," Yuke said.

"Yeah," I said. "What are we going to do about it?"

"Well, I don't know," he said. "First, let's see what we found out."

"We know those guys are stealing cars," I said. "We should tell the police about that."

"We can't do that," Yuke said.

"Why not?"

"Because there's something else we know," he said. "We know Phil is mixed up in it. And we're pretty sure he doesn't want to be."

"Yeah," I said. "It sounded like that guy was making him relay messages."

"I wonder why he's doing it," Yuke asked.

"I guess the guy has something on him," I answered.

"You're probably right. Do you think we can find out what it is?"

"How can we do that?"

"I don't know," Yuke said. "And here's another question we can't answer. Does Phil know what those guys are doing? Or is he just taking messages from one guy and sending them to another?"

"I still think we should call the police," I said.

"Maybe you're right," Yuke said.

"Come on. Let's do it right now."

"Wait," Yuke said. "Let's talk it out."

So we talked. We kept going over the same things. We knew Phil was helping them. But we were pretty sure he was being forced to do it. If we called the police, he would be arrested. And he was only as old as we were. It didn't seem right to have a kid our age arrested.

So we agreed not to call the police yet. But we would have to do something.

"We have to find out more about the setup," Yuke said.

"Well," I said, "I'll tell you one thing. I'm not going back to that warehouse. Nothing could get me into that place again."

Yuke smiled and said, "Me neither. We came too close to getting caught last night. No, we'll have to find out about it some other way."

"Maybe we can pick up another conversation," I said.

Yuke thought for a few seconds. Then he said, "I guess we should try that. I can't think of any other way of getting information. We'll try to listen to Phil and Slim talking again."

We went into Yuke's house. First, we tried listening in, to see if we could pick up a conversation. There was nothing going on.

Then we called Phil. He answered. He

remembered talking to Yuke a few days before.

"How are things going?" Yuke asked.

"Oh, pretty good," Phil said. "Most of my friends are away on vacation. So things are pretty quiet."

"Say, listen," Yuke said, "is everything all right? I mean, is anything wrong?"

"What do you mean?" Phil asked.

"Oh, nothing, really," Yuke said. "I just wondered if anything was wrong. I thought you might need some help or something."

I guess Yuke was trying to be clever. He didn't want to mention the stolen cars. But he was trying to get Phil to talk about them. So far, he was doing a lousy job.

"What kind of help?" Phil asked. He sounded like he was getting angry.

"Listen, Phil," Yuke said, "I think I'd better just tell you. My friend and I were trying to call you yesterday. His name's Greg. He's here now. We overheard you talking to Slim. You sounded scared or something. So we checked out that theater you were talking about —"

Phil yelled, "You did what?"

"Wait a minute," Yuke said. "I told you, we want to help. We went to the theater on West Street last night and saw the show."

"OK," Phil said. "What do you guys want? I don't have any money. So you can call the cops if you want to."

"No," Yuke said, "you've got it wrong. I was trying to tell you before. We want to know if we can help you."

"I don't know how you can," Phil said. "Listen, we had better sign off."

"Wait," Yuke said, "don't sign off yet. Can we meet you someplace? Maybe we can talk about it."

Phil said, "I told you to call the cops if you want to."

"We don't want to," Yuke said. "Where can we meet you?"

"OK," Phil said. "You know the drugstore on the corner of Franklin and Park?"

Yuke looked at me. I nodded.

"Yes," Yuke said, "we know."

"Meet me there in half an hour," Phil said.

After they signed off, Yuke said, "That is one very scared guy."

"I know," I said. "He thinks we're trying to blackmail him."

"We'll just have to convince him that we want to help him out. Let's go."

We rode off to Franklin and Park.

CHAPTER 8

It took us about 20 minutes to get to the drugstore. It was a pretty busy place. We chained our bikes outside. Then we looked in the drugstore. There were three people sitting in a booth, eating ice cream.

"I just thought of something," I said.

"What?" Yuke asked.

"How are we going to know Phil?" I said. "We don't even know what he looks like."

"That's right," he said. "I never thought of that."

But we had no trouble spotting him. He came in as we were talking. He looked from side to side. He seemed very scared. We knew it was Phil.

Yuke walked up to him and said, "Phil?"

Phil moved back a step. "Yes," he said, "I'm Phil. Who are you?"

Yuke held out his hand. "I'm Yuke," he said. Phil looked at Yuke's hand for a second. Then he shook it. Yuke said, "This is Greg. He knows all about this too."

I shook hands with Phil. "Hi," I said. "You want to sit at one of those tables over there?"

We went to a table and sat down. A waitress came over. We all ordered root beer. Then the waitress left.

"Listen, Phil," Yuke said. "First, let us explain something to you. We're not trying to get you into any trouble."

"I'm already in trouble," Phil said.

"We figured that," I said. "But we want to help you."

"How do you plan to do that?" Phil asked.

"We don't know yet," Yuke said. "First, we

have to know what kind of trouble you're in."

"I thought you knew about it," Phil said.

"We know you're sending messages for car thieves," Yuke said. "But we don't know how you got mixed up in it."

Phil said, "Sometimes I wonder about that myself. I've never done anything like this before. You guys have to believe me."

"We believe you," Yuke said. "Tell us about it."

"I guess I might as well," Phil said. "You know the worst part already."

The waitress brought our drinks. When she left, Phil took a deep breath. Then he started talking.

"About six months ago," he said, "I used to go around with these guys from my street. They were kind of a rough crowd. You know, a gang fight now and then, that kind of thing. A guy named Slim was sort of in charge of things."

I said, "That's the guy you were talking to on the radio."

"That's right," Phil said. "He's about 20 years old. He was the leader. Well, I got into some shoplifting with these guys. It was nothing big. But we did it three or four times a week."

"What kinds of things did you take?" Yuke asked.

Phil said, "Mostly things like records and shirts. Small things from stores. I did it for two or three months. We would take the stuff and

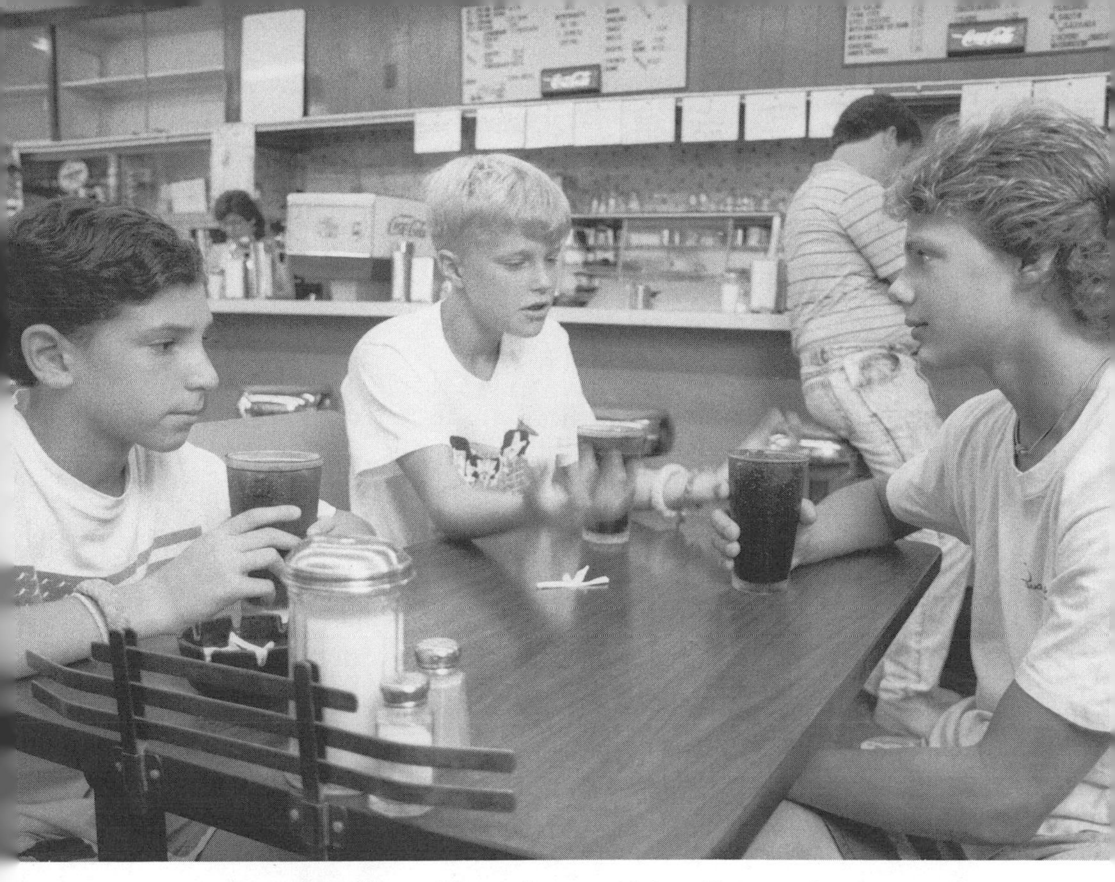

give it to Slim. Then he would sell it and give us some of the money."

Phil took a sip of his root beer. "After a while," he said, "I told Slim I wanted to quit. I was getting scared. One of the guys was arrested. He didn't tell the cops anything about the rest of us. But it scared me."

"What did Slim say?" I asked. "I mean, when you told him you were quitting."

"He said I couldn't do it," Phil said. "He said he would call my father. He would tell my father what I had been doing."

"So you kept working for him?" Yuke asked.

"Yes," Phil said. "Then, about a month ago,

Slim told me he had a new job. He was giving up shoplifting. He was tied up with some big-time people. And he said I had to use my radio to help him."

"Why can't he get the messages by phone?" I said.

"He's crazy about radios. In fact, I think he's just crazy. Every time I asked him why use the radios he had a different answer. Once he said he thought his phone was tapped. Another time he said he had seen a spy movie where they used radios. So he wanted to use radios too. I don't think he really had a good reason. It's like I told you, I think he's crazy!"

"Why didn't you just refuse to help him?" I asked. "What could he do?"

"He would tell my father about the shoplifting," Phil said.

"So you're being blackmailed," Yuke said.

"That's right," Phil said. "And there's no way I can get out of it."

"What happens if your father finds out?" I asked.

Phil thought for a few seconds. "I'm not sure," he said. "I guess I'm just too scared to want to find out. So I've been doing what Slim tells me to do."

"I think the time has come to find out," Yuke said. "I think you had better tell him yourself."

Phil stared into his glass. "Well," he said,

"I've been thinking about doing that. So far, I haven't had the nerve."

"You're going to have to tell the police, too," Yuke said.

"I know," Phil said. "But you know what I would really like to do? I would like to have those guys caught with the stolen cars."

Nobody said anything for a while. Then Yuke's face broke into a big smile.

"What is there to smile about?" Phil asked him.

"I have a plan," Yuke said.

"A plan for what?" I asked.

"A plan to catch those guys red-handed!"

"I don't want to get you guys involved in this," Phil said. "It's bad enough that I'm in trouble."

"Are you kidding?" Yuke said. "I wouldn't let you do it without us. We're already involved in it. Right, Greg?"

"Yeah," I said, "I guess so." I didn't really want to get mixed up in any plan. But Yuke was all excited. So I decided to go along.

"You know," Phil said, "I really trust you." He wasn't talking to both of us. He was talking to Yuke.

Yuke smiled at him. "Good," he said. "There's no reason why you shouldn't trust us."

"Yes, there is," Phil said. "There are plenty of reasons. But I just wanted you to know that I really trust you."

Yuke seemed a little embarrassed. But I knew just what Phil meant. Yuke was the kind of guy anybody could trust. Nobody said anything for a few seconds. Then Yuke cleared his throat and started talking again.

"The first thing to do," he said, "is tell your father. No, wait. Don't do that. Tell him after we get these guys arrested."

"Arrested?" Phil asked. "How are we going to do that?"

"It's all going to happen tomorrow," Yuke said. "Now, here's my plan."

We spent the next half hour listening to Yuke.

CHAPTER 9

The next day was the slowest day of my life. We had to wait until four o'clock. We would start our plan then. Yuke and I kept checking the time all day long. It seemed as if four o'clock would never come.

We spent part of the afternoon playing basketball. At three, Yuke said we had better go home and get ready. Then we saw Jamie Roberts. He was with three of his friends.

Jamie walked up to us. He said to Yuke, "Hello, new kid. Where are you going in such a hurry?"

Yuke stopped walking. "Look," he said, "I don't know who you are. But I don't have time for you right now."

"That's what you said the last time," Jamie said. "That excuse won't work twice." He pushed Yuke to the ground.

I started to move toward Jamie. Two of his friends held me back. "Private fight," one of them said. "Just the two of them."

I didn't want them to fight. We had to get home. Phil was going to need us to trap those car thieves. But there wasn't anything I could do to stop this fight.

Yuke got up from the ground. "OK," he said. "If we have to, I guess we have to." He swung at Jamie.

Jamie blocked the punch. Then he threw a left

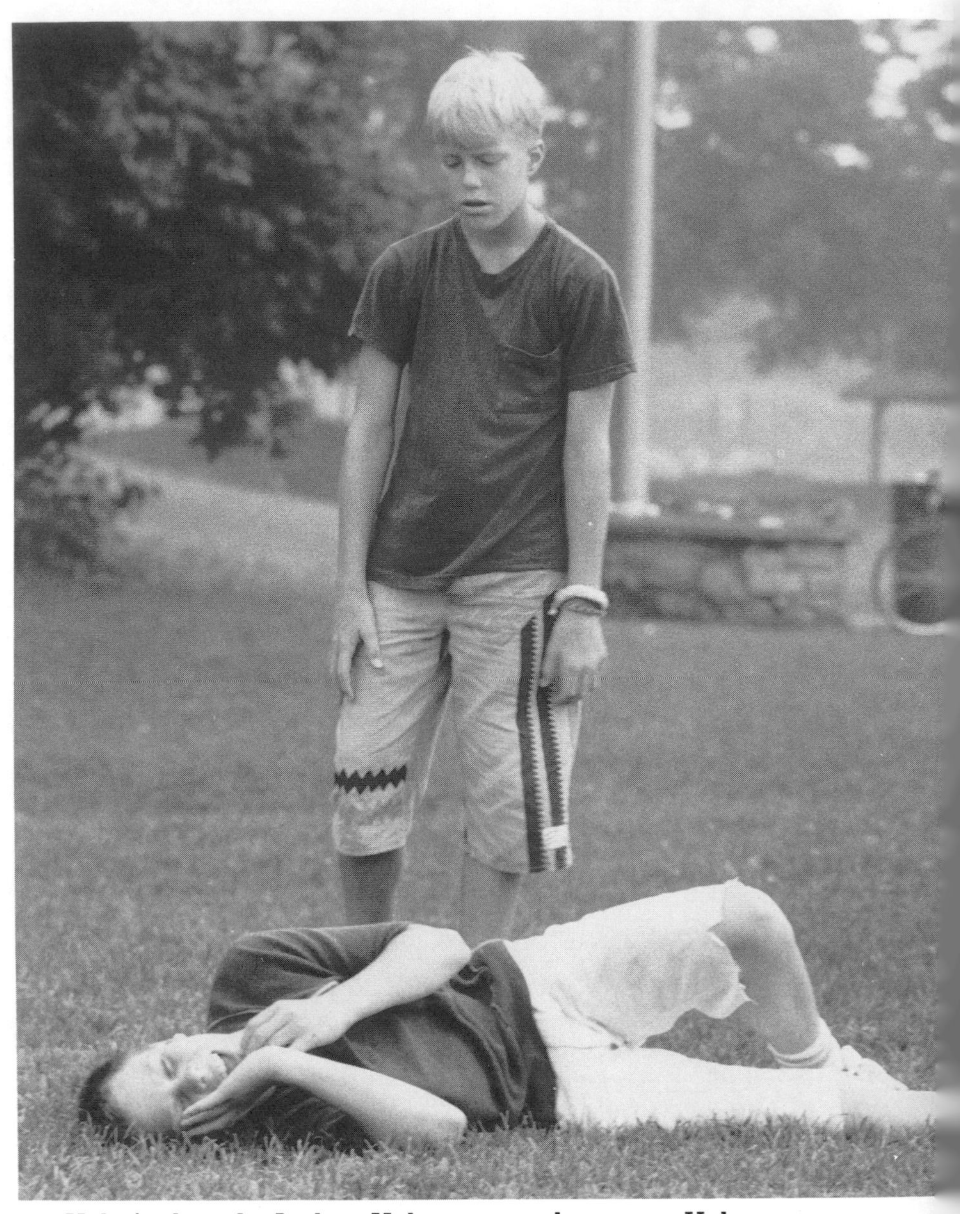

at Yuke's head. It hit Yuke near the ear. Yuke backed off and shook his head a little. Then he charged. He hit Jamie in the stomach, then on the side of the chin. Jamie lost his balance and fell. Yuke stood still, waiting for him to get up.

"That's enough, you guys," a voice said. It was the park supervisor. We all looked over at him. He was only a college guy. But he was big, maybe 225 pounds. And way over six feet.

He stepped between Yuke and Jamie. "Do your

fighting someplace else," he said.

Nobody was about to argue with him. Yuke stepped around him and walked past Jamie. Jamie and his friends walked behind us as we went toward our bikes.

"Next time, new kid," Jamie said. "There's going to be a next time."

Yuke just kept walking. He didn't say anything. We got on our bikes and rode away.

"He'll try again," I said.

"No, he won't," Yuke said. "That was a good pair of punches I gave him. I think he got the point."

I thought about that. It was only two punches. But I had to agree. They weren't the kind of punches you usually see in a street fight. They were more like movie punches. But I don't think they felt like movie punches. I think they felt real. Maybe Yuke was right. Maybe Jamie would go looking for other targets from now on.

"Let's go," Yuke said. He put on a burst of speed, and I followed. We had some important work to do. And we didn't want to be late. We got to his room at 3:30.

I forgot all about the fight. I forgot about everything except what we were going to do. I was nervous, and scared, and excited.

Yuke sat down at the radio. He smiled at me. "Ready?" he said.

"Ready," I said. "I hope it works."

CHAPTER 10

We tuned in on Phil. He had to carry out the first part of the plan. We waited a couple of minutes. Then we heard him calling Slim. When Slim answered, Phil made believe he was all excited.

"I'm having trouble with my radio," Phil said. "I've been trying to get you for 20 minutes!"

"Well, you've got me," Slim said. "What's up?"

"It took me so long, I don't have time to explain," Phil said. "Just get all the actors. Tell them to bring their props to the theater. Tell them to get there right away!"

"What are you talking about?" Slim asked. "We weren't supposed to go there until tomorrow."

"Get going!" Phil yelled. "You're already late!"

Phil cut him off. Then I crossed my fingers. If Slim called Phil back, there would be trouble. He would ask a lot of questions. Then he would find out that Phil was lying.

We waited a few minutes. Slim didn't call him. That meant he believed Phil about not having any time to waste. It also meant he was getting the drivers together.

"Let's go!" Yuke said.

We ran downstairs and hopped on our bikes. The next step had to be done fast. We rode to the shopping center. Yuke hopped off his bike and went to a public phone. We had to call

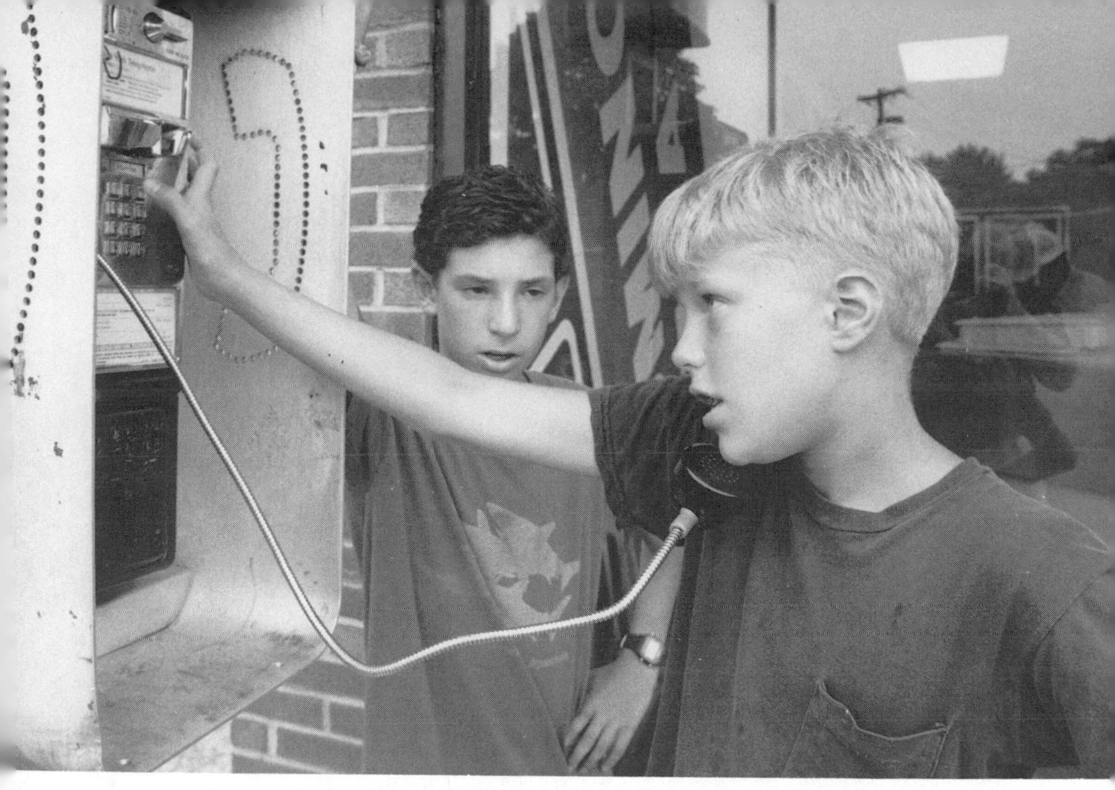

the police. We couldn't do it from his house. We didn't want his mother to hear.

"Is this the police department?" Yuke asked. "Listen, you have to get some squad cars to 613 West Street. You have to do it right away. A ring of car thieves will be there in a few minutes. Every one of them will be driving a stolen car."

Yuke listened for a few seconds to the voice on the other end. Then he said, "No, I can't give you my name. Just get the squad cars there. And tell them to park a few blocks away from the place."

Then he hung up the phone.

"Come on," he said, "let's go watch the show."

"Wait a minute," I said. "Why didn't you give them your name?"

He smiled at me. "I'll bet you know why," he said.

I smiled back, and said, "Yeah, I guess I do. Phil needs the publicity."

"You're learning," he said. "You're learning fast." And we took off for the warehouse. On the way there, I did some thinking. Sure, I knew why Yuke didn't give the police his name. He wanted

Phil to get the credit when the whole thing was over. That didn't surprise me.

But something else did surprise me. I was surprised that I felt the same way as Yuke. A week earlier, I would have killed anybody who tried to take credit for something I had done. But Yuke made that seem stupid.

With Yuke around, it was enough to do

something exciting. It didn't matter if people ever knew you did it. It was nice to believe something like that. It made me stop worrying about a lot of silly things that used to bother me.

When we got to the warehouse, the place was closed. There were three drivers sitting in their cars. They were parked in front of the big door. We stayed in a doorway across the street.

In a few minutes, three more cars pulled up. A skinny guy got out of one of them and banged on the warehouse door.

"What's up, Slim?" one driver said to the skinny guy. "I thought they'd be waiting for us."

"Me too," Slim said. "The kid said to get here right away."

"Where are the cops?" I asked Yuke.

"I don't know," he said. "Maybe they didn't believe me."

One of the other drivers said to Slim, "Maybe that kid is lying."

Slim laughed. "Him?" he said. "He's too scared. He's also too dumb to make up something like that." Slim was still laughing when he heard the loudspeaker:

"This is the police," the voice said. "All of you stay right where you are. The block is surrounded."

Slim and the other drivers looked around. Then Slim started to run. Three policemen stepped out of a doorway at the end of the block. They had their guns drawn. Slim stopped.

"All of you get against that wall," the voice said. "Put your hands on the wall, and your face down!"

The drivers stood against the wall. Policemen came out all over the block. I don't know where they had been hiding. There were about 30 of them.

We watched as the police searched the drivers. Then a patrol wagon pulled up, and all of the drivers climbed in. By this time, there were reporters and photographers all over the block.

"The fun's over," Yuke said. "Let's get out of here." We started walking to where we had left our bikes. Then we heard a voice.

"Hey, you two. What are you doing here?"

We stopped and turned around. It was a policeman.

"We were just going to get our bikes," Yuke said. "We were riding around. We stopped to see what all the noise was about."

"Get going," the policeman said. "This is no place for a couple of kids."

We both smiled. We jumped on our bikes and rode home.

That night, we called Phil. Yuke told him to tell his father the whole story. He said Phil should take credit for calling the police. He didn't want anybody to know we had been part of the plan.

Phil didn't understand. He wanted us to get our names in the papers or something. But Yuke told him to leave us out of it.

But I understood. And I agreed with Yuke. We didn't have too much to gain by taking credit. Sure, it would have been nice to be treated like heroes. But Phil had to prove that he wouldn't get mixed up in this kind of thing again. So it was important for him to get as much credit as he could.

So Yuke and I kept it a secret. It was enough to know that we had done it. We didn't need a pat on the back from anybody.

The story made headlines in the papers. There was even a little piece on the six o'clock news. Phil had his name mentioned on the news. And his picture was in the papers.

So, the next day, everybody was talking about it. Pete and Benny were pretty excited about the whole thing.

"Boy," Pete said, "nothing like that ever happens to us."

"Yeah," Benny said. "Hey, Yuke, how come you

don't get calls like that on your radio?"

Yuke smiled. "Some guys are just lucky," he said. "All I ever get is people who want to talk about the weather."

"Yeah," Benny said. "Life sure is dull around here."

It would have been nice to tell them. But it was better just to smile and say, "Yeah. Dull."